DRAMA,
DRINKS
AND
DOUBLE
FAULTS

W9-AZJ-536

The skinny
about tennis fanatics that
no one has had the *balls* to say . . . 'til now!

Accolades!

"An entertaining, unfiltered look at the players in women's league tennis that could only be offered by another female player."
    Michael McFarlane
    Head Pro and Co-Owner
    Shadow Mountain Resort
    Palm Desert, CA

"A lighthearted and entertaining insight into the world of women's league play."
    Rhona Kaczmarczyk
    2005 USPTA Player of the Year
    2010 USTA #1 national rank
        and inducted into Colorado Tennis Hall of Fame

DRAMA, DRINKS AND DOUBLE FAULTS

Mary Moses

Littleton, Colorado
www. WhatAboutTennis.com

Copyright © 2014 by Mary Moses

All rights reserved. No part of this book may be used or reproduced, distributed, or transmitted in any form or by any means, including photocopying, recording, or other electronic or mechanical methods, without the written permission of the publisher, except in the case of brief quotations embodied in critical reviews and certain other noncommercial uses permitted by copyright law. For permission requests, write to the publisher addressed at the address below.

While the author has made every effort to provide accurate Internet information at the time of publication, neither the publisher nor the author assume any responsibility for errors, or for changes that occur after publication. Further, the publisher does not have any control over and does not assume any responsibiity for author or third party websites or their content.

What About Tennis?
7944 S. Bemis St.
Littleton, CO 80120
303-522-7718
www.DramaDrinksandDoubleFaults.com

Printed in the United States of America.

ISBN: 978-0-615-96561-1

Editor: Keren Kilgore
Interior and cover design: Lightning Tree Creative Media
Artist: Rick Menard

Dedication

To my dear friend, Linda Schley.
Without your encouragement, enthusiasm,
and true selflessness, this book
would have never been possible.

Acknowledgements

To all those intense, insatiable,
and utterly incredible women who gave me inspiration
for this book each and every time you stepped on the court.
You're all a bit crazy, and I wouldn't have it any other way.

Contents

Welcome 11

One of Those Days! 17

It's Just a Numbers Game. 21

    2.5 – "Naïve. Innocent. Trusting." 23

    3.0 – "I am not a 2.5. I am not a 2.5." 25

    3.5 – "I really should be a 4.0." 27

    4.0 – "If I could be a 4.0 forever . . . ." 29

    4.5 – "I could *never* play 4.0 again." 31

    5.0 – "It's just not good tennis at 4.5." 33

Tennis Typology 35

    Blah. Blah. Blah. 39

    The Human Backboard 41

    Hard and Harder 43

    B.A.R.B.I.E. 45

    Jekyll and Hyde 47

    Pony 49

    Bionic Woman 51

    Put a Sock In It! 53

    Alexis 55

    One and Done! 57

    Vanilla 59

    The Closet Addict 61

Laughing At Yourself 63

Typology Cocktails 67

   The Blah, Blah, Blah (White Wine Spritzer).......................... 69

   The Human Backboard (The Slow Drain) 71

   The Hard and Harder (The Raging Bull)............................... 73

   The B.A.R.B.I.E. (Skinny Cosmopolitan).............................. 75

   The Jekyll and Hyde (The Local Loco)................................ 77

   The Pony (Shirley Temple with a Kick) 79

   The Bionic Woman (The Painkiller) 81

   The Put a Sock In It (The Zipper) 83

   The Alexis (Colorado Bulldog) 85

   The One and Done (The Spicy Drunk) 87

   The Vanilla (Vanilla Lemon Drop) 89

   The Closet Addict (The Blindside) 91

Quotes 92

About the Author 95

The thing that is really hard,
and really amazing is giving up
on being perfect and beginning the work of
becoming yourself.

Anna Quindlen'

I don't want to get to the end of my life and find that I lived just the length of it. I want to have lived the width of it as well.

Diane Ackerman[2]

Welcome

Four profanities, three snide remarks, two cat fights, an overhead to the chest, and that's only the first set. Just an average day in women's social tennis—a day that we live for, dream about, and literally count down until we can go right back into "battle" again. You gave birth to your children, survived the newborn and toddler years, and successfully launched them off to school, (and girlfriend, if that doesn't deserve a nice glass of Pinot, then I don't know what does). Ultimately, after giving of yourself as a wife, mother, daughter, and friend, there comes a time when it is deserved and frankly, necessary, for us as women to have our time, our *thing*, and tennis has become that *thing*.

Tennis is one of the fastest growing women's competitive sports in the United States. Why? For the cute outfits...the cocktails with your friends after a match...and just to get out of the house. If you are reading this book, you either *are* one of these women, *know* one of these women, or *secretly desire to be* one of these women. Some of you played sports growing up as a child. Others have never been involved in an organized sport in your life besides sitting your soccer-mom butt on the sidelines, sipping a Starbucks, and bitching about the ref who didn't call off-sides (as if you actually knew what off-sides was?!).

Sometimes the strongest women
are the ones who love beyond all faults,
cry behind closed doors and fight battles
that nobody knows about.

Anonymous[3]

Well, one of the unique aspects of this crazy sport is that no matter what category you find yourself in, it's okay. You can learn to play tennis at any age, without a single athletic bone in your body, and find a place where you belong—a *home*. The women who start off as your teammates can become some of your best friends and eventually a support system that you could never imagine being without.

They stand by you through the good, the bad, and the ugly, and some of those days can be quite ugly. I've experienced some of life's biggest challenges while being a part of my women's tennis team, and thankfully I can say that a teammate offering a hug, an ear to listen and one giant glass of wine never failed to help get me through.

Luckily, in spite of all those dark days, your tennis teammates will also be part of some of your biggest and brightest days. These ladies are right by your side, screaming, cheering, and popping the cork for the best events of your life. They celebrate the birth of your children (even better, the birth of your *grandchildren*). They are ecstatic upon hearing that your daughter is getting married or that your son is going to be a father. They toast your birthday, job promotion, or the fact that your second grader just got an award in the school art show. They are always looking for a reason to celebrate—and none of these celebrations would have been quite as big or as bright without. . . your "girls."

If you want something you've never had,
you must be willing to do something
you've never done.

Thomas Jefferson[4]

Not only are your "girls" there to comfort you and celebrate with you, they are also there to accept you just as you are—wrinkles, saggy boobs, and all. Besides, who else will witness you on the court losing your mind and moments later accept you with open arms as they raise their wine glasses to toast your ridiculous behavior? An amazing and frustrating fact about us is that we don't all fit into a box. We come in many shapes, sizes, abilities, and personalities, but the common factor that unites us is our love for the game. That passion keeps us coming back for more: more matches, more drills, more fights, more hugs, more victories, more losses, more drama, more drinks, more double faults, and absolutely more fun!

Our shelves are filled with self-help books, sports psychology books, and books helping us improve our tennis skills, but we are still missing something. There is no book that exposes us for who we are and then reassures us that it's okay. "Exposes me?" you ask defensively. As author Jennifer Salaiz so poignantly stated, "How 'bout a shot of truth in that denial cocktail?" Well, belly up sisters, because the bar is now open!

Being happy doesn't mean that everything is perfect. It means that you've decided to look beyond the imperfections.

Gerard Way

One of Those Days!

You see piles of laundry everywhere . . . except where laundry should be. On the way to the bus stop, your fourth grader announced that she now hates the school lunches and wants to have a lunch box packed from this day forward. You made a trip to the grocery store late last night because at bedtime your darling little first grader mentioned that he volunteered you to make a "homemade" apple pie for tomorrow's Teacher Appreciation Day. To top it off, you find yourself at the bus stop for afternoon pick up wearing the same pajama bottoms and sweatshirt that you wore in the morning because you really had nothing to do *outside* the house today.

The fact is that each one of us has been there. No matter how much we experience success at our job, adore our families, and live for those neighborhood Bunco Nights, there has to be something more—something that allows us to be a healthier, happier, and more complete version of ourselves. Thinking back, you may have noticed those ladies in your neighborhood, at your child's school, or even driving by the tennis courts on your way to run errands. You know, the ones who are skipping around in their cute tennis outfits, laughing with other tennis players, and looking refreshed and fulfilled while you, of course, are having "one of those days."

The only difference between
a rut and a grave
are the dimensions.

Ellen Glasgow[6]

If you are one of the truly fortunate ones who have discovered this psychotic, tumultuous, and self-defining sport, then I applaud you and celebrate with you. However, if you are one of the unfortunate ones who hasn't, then get your sorry ass off the couch and get moving. Now is the time to say, "This is it. This is the day that I am going to go out and find that *thing*."

One day of practice is like one day of clean living. It doesn't do any good.

Abe Lemmons[7]

It's Just a Numbers Game

If you are reading this book, it means you are a part of this crazy world of women's league tennis or ready to embark on the journey. As Lao Tzu once said, "The journey of a thousand miles begins with a single step."

After meeting a pro, hitting an endless amount of balls, and being slapped with a number (affectionately called a "rating"), you are now a part of the club. Yes, you have a number. I have a number. The world is saturated with numbers, which of course, we as women *despise*: our age, our height, our weight, our income, and (at times more importantly) our tennis rating.

You will find yourself fighting persistently, incessantly, and at the expense of others to either maintain your rating or improve it. When someone finds out that you play tennis, the very first question they inevitably ask is, "What level do you play?" That single answer lays the foundation for your self-esteem, value and over-all position in the food chain of women's league tennis. Keep in mind, the glorious and yet gut wrenching reality is that your rating can (and most likely will) change, which can place you on a pedestal or unfortunately knock you to your knees in no time at all. Sit up straight, stop nursing that cocktail and let's get down to business.

*It's not about being better than someone else;
it's about being better than you were
the day before.*

Unknown[8]

2.5

"Naïve. Innocent. Trusting."

You have started with the best of intentions—to get exercise and to make some friends. Soon your eyes will be opened, along with your pocketbook, and within weeks you will realize that you have to pay to play.

Pay the clothing vendors because at this level everything has to match, and I mean EVERYTHING: the skirt, top, shoes, socks, visor, racquet, and racquet bag.

Pay the teaching pros because like crack, one hit and you want more, need more. And let's be honest, you can't get any worse.

Pay the sitter because who else is going to watch your kids while you feed your new found addiction?

One of the most courageous things
you can do is identify yourself,
know who you are, what you believe in
and where you want to go.

Sheila Murray Bethel

3.0

"I am not a 2.5. I am not a 2.5."

Simply put, 3.0s are just thankful to not be 2.5s any longer and are desperate to keep it that way. Pre-match warm up means showing up to practice at least an hour prior to playing, and if a teammate makes the critical error of not showing up that early, then she can kiss goodbye any chance of making the line-up for a while.

Captains start dipping their little virgin toes into the cesspool of recruiting, seeking out singles players (ANY singles players) and doubles players who can manage to play together and hopefully stay together, avoiding the drama-filled "doubles divorce."

*Too many people over value
what they are not
and under value what they are.*

Malcolm S. Forbes[10]

3.5

"I really should be a 4.0."

Squatters! This level has the largest number of players that will get to 3.5 and stay at 3.5 for a very long time, if not for the rest of their tennis playing days. Some are absolutely thrilled to plant their happy asses here with no intentions of ever advancing. However, there is also the resentful, sniveling, whiner who walks around with a huge chip on her shoulder because according to her calculations, she should have been moved up to 4.0 years ago. Get a grip!

Perseverance is not a long race;
it is many short races one after the other.

Walter Elliott"

4.0

"If I could be a 4.0 forever . . . ."

Yes Ma'am! You have finally broken out of the 3.5 abyss, but don't be getting all drunk with elation quite yet. One bonehead match and you will find yourself right back at 3.5, and you can't tell me you aren't losing sleep over that thought!

Captain is now more than just a hollow title. Because she now has real responsibilities, she is starting to complain about her thankless job of "running" the team, yet she secretly has nightmares about other players taking control.

The two things you can count on are that singles players will be as heavily recruited as LeBron James before he took his talents to South Beach, and doubles partners are recycled or simply thrown away like empty bottles of Chardonnay.

Competition brings out the best in products and the worst in people.

David Sarnoff[12]

4.5

"I could never play 4.0 again."

This is the lowest level in which you will find ex-college players, so expect plenty of bitching. Complaints are imminent from the player who gets stuck playing her. "I can't believe I have to play the college kid." "Why is she playing this level? It can't be fun for her." "There is no way she is only a 4.5!" Funny how the complaints magically disappear once you are blessed with her addition to **your team**. Hypocrisy: the spice of life!

If I only had a little humility,
I would be perfect.

Ted Turner[13]

5.0

"It's just not good tennis at 4.5."

There are a few things to keep in mind about 5.0s. First, is the attire. The unwritten rule of thumb is the worse the clothes, the better the player. You have more players showing up for matches in an old t-shirt or tank top and a pair of old shorts than you do wearing an actual tennis top and skirt. Secondly, in sharp contrast to the 3.0s, be surprised if they aren't any more than 15 minutes late to start the match. You are supposed to feel fortunate that their cocky asses even showed up at all. Thirdly, the days of hanging out, hosting, or spending any sort of time together after your match is virtually non-existent. You play. YOU BETTER WIN. You go home.

How does that cocktail taste now? Going down a little harsh? Too strong? Well, get your big girl panties on. Though happy hour may be over, the evening has only just begun. Belly up a little closer and listen carefully, because the next round is on me!

Everything we do we choose.
So what is there to regret?
You are the person you chose to be.

Paul Arden[14]

Tennis Typology

Now prepare yourself for initiation, ladies. The main piece after officially becoming a member of this underworld and being given a rating is figuring out who you are . . . or should I say **what** you are. As much as you don't fit into a box, the fact is that you will be affixed with a label bestowed upon you by women who know nothing about you, yet consider themselves the experts looking into the deepest, darkest crevices of your being, commonly referred to as **your opponents**.

Wake-up call # 1: You have been labeled.

Wake-up call # 2: Your label is NOT good. If it was, then what's the point of labeling?

Wake-up call # 3: As much as you may want to change your label, forget about it. Like a first impression, it never goes away.

If you are wondering why this labeling process is necessary, then it's apparent you haven't stepped foot on a court in true competition. This process is necessary because it makes us feel better about ourselves, and isn't that why we play, ladies?

The truth will set you free.
But first, it will piss you off.

Gloria Steinem[15]

Now, for those of you who have played, these labels will not be a surprise. You admit they are accurate, and yet with reluctance agree that without each one of them, the "experience" would not be the same. You may avoid them as individuals, but realize that each one is an essential ingredient for the recipe of women's league tennis. What's a dirty martini without the olives, right?

He that is good for making excuses is seldom good for anything else.

Benjamin Franklin[17]

Blah. Blah. Blah.

"Gosh, I haven't hit a ball in 2 weeks." "The sun was in my eyes." "The players on the other court were distracting me." Blah. Blah. Blah. We all know the type. She always has an excuse. She always has a reason, and it certainly is never that she was simply *outplayed*. She can come across as quiet, pouty, and lacking confidence, but don't you dare fall victim to that load of crap. She will whine about how poorly she is playing while secretly giving you absolutely no credit for the win. The seed is planted at the changeover with a comment or a groan. "I really should get that knee surgery that I need" or "my youngest was throwing up all night." It ends at the net shaking hands. "Nice playing. Sorry I didn't give you a good match today. I just didn't get much sleep last night." Blah! Blah! Blah!

The depressing thing about tennis
is that no matter how good I get,
I'll never be as good as a wall.

Mitch Hedberg[16]

The Human Backboard

The common thought associated with playing this type of player is, "I want to shoot myself!" This incredibly ugly version of tennis is often overlooked and underestimated and as a result, it's successful. This inevitably leads her opponent to the next commonly thought phrase, "I should just quit tennis!" She plants her ass at the baseline, strolls around effortlessly, and gets every ball back *exactly* where it should go and *exactly* where you are not. Adding salt to the wound, this player comes off the court utterly astonished that she won. Bullsh*t! She knows her game, she knows it works, and she has absolutely no intentions of changing it ... *ever*.

There are two kinds of egotists:
those who admit it, and the rest of us.

Laurence J. Peter [18]

Hard and Harder

It doesn't matter if the ball goes in. It doesn't matter if it takes someone's head off, just as long as she hits the sh*t out of it. Not only does she fail to realize that other players are neither impressed nor intimidated by her power, but she also refuses to acknowledge any opponent who doesn't try to hit the ball equally as hard. This player is constantly heard coming off the court belittling her opponents that played "dink ball." Well, wake up sister, because those opponents who just played "dink ball" against you, just WON.

Big boobs don't make women stupid.

They make men stupid.

Anonymous[19]

B.A.R.B.O.E.
(Boobs Aren't Real. Botox In Excess.)

She's bustin' out of her tennis top, her skirt covers less than half of what it should, and her face has had more botox injections than the Real Housewives of Beverly Hills. As she parades her collagen-filled ass and lips all over the court, all you can wonder is exactly how long did it take her to squeeze into that stripper outfit?!

The mark of great sportsmen is not how
good they are at their best,
but how good they are at their worst.

Martina Navratilova[20]

Jekyll and Hyde

This opponent can actually make you feel like the crazy one. She is overly gracious in the warm-up, cracks jokes, and gives you plenty of compliments. How-ever, once the warm-up is over, the good will from just minutes earlier is out the window. Instead, she constantly questions your calls, gives you the cold shoulder on the change-overs, and uses you and your partner's head for target practice throughout the match.

Eventually, the last point of your "Sybil" match is over. If she lost, there's a hesitant handshake, no eye contact and a half-assed "nice match." What's even more nauseating are her antics if she won: a giant bear hug, followed up by "you played so well!" or "you were on fire today!" Later she endlessly repeats to everyone how well you played and how she can't believe she beat you. My recommendation: that giant, nasty pill to swallow needs to be followed up with one big ass chaser. Uuuuggghhh!

To be old and wise
you must first be young and stupid.

Anonymous[21]

Pony

Pony tail required and the higher the better. This term is commonly associated with the early twenty-somethings. They be-bop their twenty-something bodies and their twenty-something brains around the court while their naturally colored, extension-free ponytails flip in the wind. The money you just spent at your hair-guy Richard's salon and on your new Lululemon outfit all goes down the toilet in a matter of seconds when the Ponies arrive on the court. However, be reassured, those Ponies won't stay Ponies forever.

We are stuck with technology
when what we really want
is just stuff that works.

Douglas Adams[22]

Bionic Woman

This player comes on the court covered from head to toe with sh*t. She's wearing every bionic invention available on the market along with every elbow sleeve, ankle support, and thigh wrap known to man. Not to mention that she reeks of Ben-Gay or Bio-Freeze. Your immediate thought after warm-up is that this match is a no-brainer since she refused to move for any ball that wasn't hit perfectly into her strike zone, and she took 10 minutes to go back and pick up balls. Once again, opponent beware, because when it really matters not only will she magically be able to poach like a Bryan Brother, but she will also be the one at the baseline running down balls that even a Pony shouldn't be able to get to.

There's a fine line between a stream of consciousness and a babbling brook to nowhere.

Dan Harmon[23]

Drama, Drinks and Double Faults

Put a Sock In It!

This opponent can never just be quiet. She has to talk at every change over and comment about every shot—in your space, in your face, on and on and on. She has to ask you about your kids, and then of course tell you about hers, and you can't help but wonder, is she nervous, insecure, or is she actually interested in my life? Who knows and who cares! Can you just put a sock in it?!

I've learned that people will forget what you said, people will forget what you did, but people will never forget how you made them feel.

Maya Angelou[24]

Alexis

This is *the* player who is so arrogant, controversial and condescending that you only need to mention her *first* name to others and need not say another word. There is really no way to prepare for what lies ahead while competing against this opponent. Wake up and watch out because her mouth can be far more lethal than her racquet. Not

only will she try to destroy the psyche of her opponents but she may even end up destroying her own partner's psyche as well. Instead of reaching down deep inside of herself and rising to the occasion with smart points and skillful shots, she will dig down deep inside of your brain and mentally pick you apart, piece by piece, comment by comment, bad call by bad call, until there is nothing more than the mere shell of your prior existence. Have fun with that one!

*Patience is the support of weakness;
impatience the ruin of strength.*

Charles Caleb Colton[25]

One and Done!

Without hesitation she hits her shot.

It's either a winner, or it's an error.

The end.

Imperfection is beauty, madness is genius and it's better to be absolutely ridiculous than to be absolutely boring.

Marilynn Monroe[26]

Vanilla

It's probably the 10th time you've played her, and you still can't remember her name. The face looks familiar, but obviously her game hasn't left an impression on you whatsoever, except for that moment during the match when you have a flash back and are suddenly reminded that you have yet to beat this lady. She is nothing scary, nothing risky, and certainly nothing special—just a very traditional, very reliable, very "vanilla" tennis player . . . who *wins*. YAWN.

It's not denial.
I'm just selective about
the reality I accept.

Bill Watterson[27]

The Closet Addict

HAVE A GREAT DAY HONEY!

I'LL BE HOME CLEANING ALL DAY.

This player sneaks off to play or drill, lies about where she is going, and when confronted, most definitely denies it. She shows up for a drill on one end of town, casually mentions that she isn't playing much, hops back in her car after the drill to frantically drive to another tennis location on the other end of town, all in hopes that no one discovers her secret life. Family trips rescheduled, anniversary celebrations delayed and children's events missed all because of this highly addictive over-the-counter drug. The most fascinating part is the effort that she takes to hide her addiction when the reality is this Closet Addict is not even remotely "in the closet" to everybody else.

You grow up the day you have your first real laugh at yourself.

Ethel Barrymore[28]

Laughing At Yourself

I'm sure some of you are quite embarrassed right now. As you read the types, you probably found yourself smiling and giggling a little. A few of these labels may have even caused you to laugh out loud thinking of some particular opponents you have played in the past. Did any make your eyes bug out, your cheeks turn red and your forehead perspire? Hit a little too close to home? Well, remember, the first step to treating this addiction is admitting it, and the final step is embracing it. Always remember that you are in a safe place when it comes to league tennis. You may have just now realized who you are, but your teammates figured it out long ago and opted to keep you around regardless. Quoting author Russell Lynes,"If you can't ignore an insult, top it; if you can't top it, laugh it off; and if you can't laugh it off, it's probably deserved."

There are only two ways to live your life.
One is as though nothing is a miracle.
The other is as though everything is a miracle.

Albert Einstein[29]

Last call, ladies! As you are sitting around the table, winding down the evening, take a look around: a Hard and Harder, a Pony, a B.A.R.B.I.E., and an Alexis all together and all truly enjoying each other. Without this crazy sport would you have chosen these women or even had the opportunity to meet them? Probably not, and yet, here you are all together as a group . . . as a team, and you think to yourself, "I have definitely found that *home*." The bottle of wine is almost gone, but the magical thing is that this life-long adventure has barely begun. Enjoy every moment, relish every point, cherish every friendship, and don't you dare let your sorry ass go down without swinging.

Typology Cocktails

When someone shows you who they are,
believe them the first time.

Maya Angelou[30]

The Blah, Blah, Blah

(White Wine Spritzer)

Ingredients: (Makes 1 serving)

½ c. club soda

1 c. white wine

Instructions:

Pour wine into glasses.

Top with club soda.

Serve immediately.

Winning means you're willing
to go longer, work harder,
and give more than anyone else.

Vince Lombardi[31]

The Human Backboard
(The Slow Drain)

Ingredients: (Makes 1 serving)

2 oz. vodka

Juice from ½ of a lime

4 blackberries

3 tsp. sugar

Crushed ice

Instructions:

Muddle lime juice, sugar, and blackberries in a glass.

Add vodka and crushed ice.

Stir well and serve.

The strokes that are prettiest
in the warm-ups
are the ugliest under pressure.

Brad Gilbert[32]

The Hard and Harder
(The Raging Bull)

Ingredients: (Makes 1 serving)

2 oz. vodka

2 oz. lemonade

1 oz. energy drink

Instructions:

Add all ingredients in a highball glass with ice.

Stir and serve.

I've had so much plastic surgery,
when I die they will donate my body
to Tupperware.

Joan Rivers[33]

The B.A.R.B.O.E.

(Skinny Cosmopolitan)

Ingredients: (Makes 1 serving)

Crushed ice

1 oz. Citron vodka

1 oz. diet or light cranberry juice

1 T. fresh lime juice

¼ oz. of Cointreau or 4 drops orange extract

2 t. sweetener

Instructions:

Fill a cocktail shaker ½ full of crushed ice, and pour in the ingredients.

Shake well.

Strain into a martini glass and serve.

One man practicing sportsmanship
is far better than a hundred teaching it.

Knute Rockne[34]

The Jekyll and Hyde
(The Local Loco)

Ingredients: (Makes 1 serving)

1 oz. Pomegranate Liqueur

2 oz. vodka

1 oz. grapefruit juice

Lemon wedge for garnish

Coarse sugar for rimming

Instructions:

Sugar rim of one highball glass.
Set it aside.

Pour the remaining
ingredients
into a cocktail
shaker with ice.

Shake and strain
into the prepared
glass.

Garnish with a
lemon wedge and
serve.

No one can make you feel inferior
without your consent.

Eleanor Roosevelt[35]

The Pony
(Shirley Temple with a Kick!)

Ingredients: (Makes 1 serving)

1 oz. vodka

5 - 6 oz. lemon-lime soda (Sprite or 7up)

1 dash grenadine syrup

Instructions:

Pour the vodka over ice cubes in a highball glass.

Fill the glass the rest of the way with lemon-lime soda.

Add grenadine, garnish with a cherry, and serve.

The question isn't
who is going to let me:
it's who is going to stop me.

Ayn Rand[36]

The Bionic Woman

(The Painkiller)

Ingredients: (Makes 1 serving)

1 oz. lite cream of coconut

1 oz. orange juice

1 oz. pineapple juice

1 oz. spiced rum

Instructions:

Fill highball glass ½ full of ice.

Pour all ingredients over ice and stir.

Serve.

It's good to shut up sometimes.

Marcel Marceau[37]

The Put a Sock in It
(The Zipper)

Ingredients: (Makes 6 servings)

2 t. sugar

1 lime wedge

3 ½ c. watermelon (cubed and seeded)

2 T. sugar

½ c. tequila

3 T. fresh lime juice

1 T. Triple Sec

Instructions:

Sugar rims of 6 highball glasses.

Combine the rest of the ingredients in a blender and process until smooth.

Fill each sugared glass with crushed ice and add ½ c. margarita to each glass.

Serve.

Don't talk about yourself;
it will be done when you leave.

Wilson Mizner[38]

The Alexis
(Colorado Bulldog)

Ingredients: (Makes 1 serving)

1 oz. vodka

1 oz. Kahlua coffee liqueur

1 ½ oz. cream

Splash of Coca-Cola

Instructions:

Pour vodka and Kahlua over ice into a highball glass.

Then pour in cream and top off with Coca-Cola and serve.

You miss 100% of the shots you don't take.

Wayne Gretzky[39]

The One and Done
(The Spicy Drunk)

Ingredients: (Makes 2-3 servings)

½ c. tequila

¼ c. orange liqueur

¼ c. lime juice

¼ c. water

¼ c. simple syrup
(equal parts water
and syrup)

4 thin slices
cucumber

4 thin slices
jalapeno

Salt for glass rims
(optional)

Instructions:

Combine all ingredients in a pitcher.

Chill for at least an hour (the longer the margarita sits, the more cucumber and jalapeno flavors infuse into the drink).

Serve over ice in salt-rimmed glasses.

Consistency is the last refuge
of the unimaginative.

Oscar Wilde[40]

The Vanilla
(Vanilla Lemon Drop)

Ingredients: (Makes 1 serving)

2 oz. lemon-lime soda (Sprite, 7-Up)

2 oz. lemonade

1 ½ oz. vanilla flavored vodka

1 oz. lemon liqueur

Ice cubes

Sliced rounds of lemon for garnish

Instructions:

Fill a highball glass with ice.

Pour lemon-lime soda, lemonade, vanilla flavored vodka and lemon liqueur into a cocktail shaker filled with ice and freshly sliced lemon rounds.

Shake and strain into highball glass with ice and serve.

Sports do not build character.

They reveal it.

John Wooden[41]

The Closet Addict
(The Blindside)

Ingredients: (Makes 1 serving)

2 oz. vodka

2 oz. orange juice

2 oz. grapefruit juice

1 oz. strawberry syrup or muddle 2-3 strawberries with 1 t. sugar

Instructions:

Pour strawberry syrup, orange juice, and grapefruit juice in a highball glass.

Add vodka, stir, add ice and serve.

Quotes

[1] Anna Quindlen. http://www.quoteswave.com/picture-quotes/106699

[2] Diane Ackerman (n.d.) http://www.goodreads.com/quotes/10429-i-don-t-want-to-get-to-the-end-of-my

[3] Anonymous. http://godisheart.blogspot.com/2013/05/sometimes-strongest-women-are-ones-who.html

[4] Thomas Jefferson. http://www.goodreads.com/quotes/374117-if-you-want-something-you-ve-never-had-you-must-b

[5] Gerard Way. http://www.goodreads.com/quotes/342325-being-happy-doesn-t-mean-that-everything-is-perfect-it-means

[6] Ellen Glasgow. http://thinkexist.com/quotation/the_only_difference_between_a_rut_and_a_grave_are/185387.html

[7] Abe Lemmons. http://www.myspacecelebquotes.com/quote/one-day-of-practice-is-like,17407.htm

[8] Unknown. http://www.boardofwisdom.com/togo/Quotes/ShowQuote?msgid=296237#.UuGW2BDn_IU

[9] Sheila Murray Bethel. http://www.searchquotes.com/quotes/author/Sheila_Murray_Bethel/

[10] Malcolm S. Forbes. http://thinkexist.com/quotation/too_many_people_overvalue_what_they_are_not_and/215014.html

[11] Walter Elliott. http://thinkexist.com/quotation/perseverance_is_not_a_long_race-it_is_many_short/168492.html

[12] David Sarnoff. http://www.goodreads.com/quotes/165198-competition-brings-out-the-best-in-products-and-the-worst

[13] Ted Turner. http://www.quotationspage.com/quote/23573.html

[14] Paul Arder. http://www.goodreads.com/quotes/942970-everything-we-do-we-choose-so-what-is-there-to

[15] Gloria Steinem. http://www.goodreads.com/quotes/11090-the-truth-will-set-you-free-but-first-it-will

[16] Mitch Hedberg. http://www.quotationspage.com/quote/38012.html

[17] Benjamin Franklin. http://www.quotationspage.com/quote/36376.html

[18] Laurence J. Peter. http://www.quotegarden.com/humility.html

[19] Martina Navratilova. http://www.brainyquote.com/quotes/authors/m/martina_navratilova.html

[20] Anonymous. http://www.searchquotes.com/quotation/Big_boobs_don't_make_a_woman_stupid._They_make_men_stupid./390915/

[21] Anonymous. http://www.boardofwisdom.com/togo/Quotes/ShowQuote?msgid=186629#.UuGcuxDn_IU

[22] Douglas Adams. http://www.notable-quotes.com/a/adams_douglas.html

[23]Dan Harmon. http://www.brainyquote.com/quotes/authors/d/dan_harmon.htm

[24]Maya Angelou. http://www.goodreads.com/quotes/5934-i-ve-learned-that-people-will-forget-what-you-said-people

[25]Charles Caleb Colton. http://www.famouslyquoted.com/charles-caleb-colton-quotes/quote-36517

[26]Marilynn Monroe. http://www.goodreads.com/quotes/6384-imperfection-is-beauty-madness-is-genius-and-it-s-better-to

[27]Bill Watterson. http://www.brainyquote.com/quotes/quotes/b/billwatter383247.html

[28]Ethel Barrymore. http://www.brainyquote.com/quotes/authors/e/ethel_barrymore.html

[29]Albert Einstein. http://www.goodreads.com/quotes/987-there-are-only-two-ways-to-live-your-life-one

[30]Maya Angelou. http://www.goodreads.com/quotes/335-the-first-time-someone-shows-you-who-they-are-believe

[31]Vince Lombardi. http://boardofwisdom.com/togo/Quotes/ShowQuote?msgid=8944#.UuGfhxDn_IU

[32]Brad Gilbert. http://www.newyorker.com/online/blogs/sportingscene/2007/08/the-golden-rule.html

[33]Joan Rivers. http://www.brainyquote.com/quotes/authors/j/joan_rivers.html

[34]Knute Rockne. http://www.brainyquote.com/quotes/quotes/k/knuterockn231974.html

[35]Eleanor Roosevelt. http://www.brainyquote.com/quotes/quotes/e/eleanorroo161321.html

[36]Ayn Rand. http://www.brainyquote.com/quotes/quotes/a/aynrand105316.html

[37]Marcel Marceau. https://www.goodreads.com/author/quotes/545217.Marcel_Marceau

[38]Wilson Mizner. http://www.brainyquote.com/quotes/authors/w/wilson_mizner.html

[39]Wayne Gretzky. https://www.goodreads.com/author/quotes/240132.Wayne_Gretzky

[40]Oscar Wilde. http://www.quotationspage.com/quote/23578.html

[41]John Wooden. http://en.thinkexist.com/quotation/sports_do_not_build_character-they_reveal_it/208017.html

About the Author

Mary has strived to be a self-proclaimed expert in raising four children, in using sarcasm in any situation, and in finding the lessons to be learned in life's biggest challenges.

She has loved tennis from the moment she picked up that wooden Rawlings racquet found in her garage at age 10, and her passion continued through high school tennis, tournament play, and eventually right up to "burn out." Unfortunately, that burn out preceded the offers she received for college tennis scholarships.

She never picked up a racquet again until just prior to having her fourth child. After all those years, she came back to find the love, thrill, and competitive spark still there, as was her old Max 200G (John McEnroe's racquet) from high school which she quickly replaced.

If her four children and the sport of tennis have taught her anything, it was the need to have a sense of humor. And thanks to the Lord's blessings, she was born with that. Her dry sarcasm keeps her sane, entertained, and constantly looking at things a little differently.

Mary lives in Littleton, Colorado where she teaches, coaches, and plays women's league tennis. Whether it's being down in the trenches with these ladies or having a front row seat for the "action," she wouldn't miss it for anything.

Well, almost anything.

CPSIA information can be obtained
at www.ICGtesting.com
Printed in the USA
FFHW010949101218
49790037-54294FF

9 780615 965611